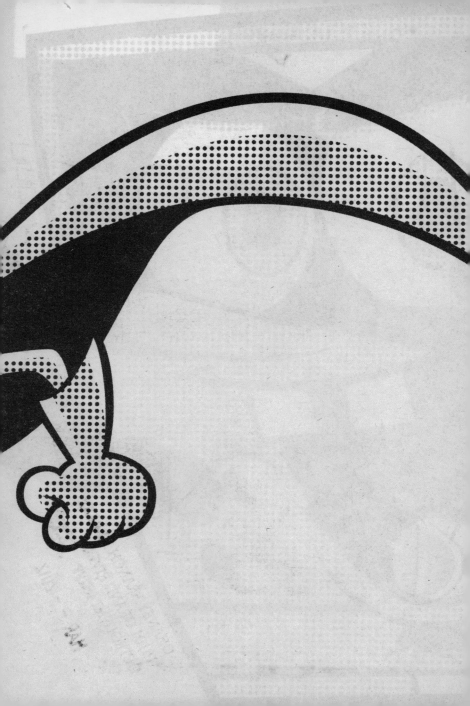

The Adventures of Man Sponge and Boy Patrick

In E.V.I.L. vs. the I.J.L.S.A.

BY ERICA DAVID | ILLUSTRATED BY THE ARTIFACT GROUP

SIMON SPOTLIGHT/NICKELODEON

NEW YORK   LONDON   TORONTO   SYDNEY   NEW DELHI

This book is a work of fiction. Any references to historical events, real people, or real locales are used fictitiously.

Other names, characters, places, and incidents are the product of the author's imagination, and any resemblance to actual events or locales or persons, living or dead, is entirely coincidental.

Based on the TV series *SpongeBob SquarePants*™ created by Stephen Hillenburg as seen on Nickelodeon™

SIMON SPOTLIGHT/NICKELODEON
An imprint of Simon & Schuster Children's Publishing Division
1230 Avenue of the Americas, New York, New York 10020

Designed by Victor Joseph Ochoa

Manufactured in the
United States of America 0112 OFF
First Edition 10 9 8 7 6 5 4 3 2 1
ISBN 978-1-4424-3584-1
Library of Congress Control Number 2011939480

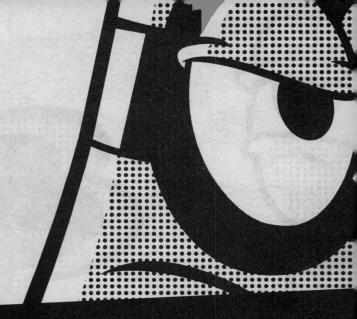

TABLE OF CONTENTS

DRIED UP

It was a beautiful morning in Bikini Bottom, but for SpongeBob SquarePants the night before had been downright ugly.

SpongeBob turned to his pet snail. "I had the worst nightmare, Gary!" he said, thinking back to his terrible dream. . . .

In the dream, SpongeBob and Patrick had been walking down the street dressed as their hero alter egos, Man Sponge and Boy Patrick. They were on the lookout for adventure. Suddenly, they noticed a jellyfish floating in the sky with a drawing taped to its side.

"Look, Pat!" Man Sponge said, pointing.

"Oh, pretty! It's a jellyfish wearing a picture of some cheese!" said Boy Patrick.

"That's not cheese! That's me! It's the Sponge Signal!" Man Sponge explained.

"That means there's trouble afoot and it's up to Man Sponge to save the day!"

"And Boy Patrick!" Patrick added. Then he scratched his head, confused. "Hey, SpongeBob, where's the Pat Signal?"

"Pat Signal? Don't be ridiculous. There isn't one," said Man Sponge. "Quickly, to the Sponge Lair!"

They ran off to the Sponge Lair—which looked a lot like SpongeBob's house. As soon as they walked in, they heard the phone ringing.

"I'll get it," Boy Patrick volunteered.

"Not so fast," Man Sponge said. He pointed to a sign stuck to the phone. "What does that say, my trusty sidekick?"

SPONGE PHONE

Boy Patrick peered at the sign. "Sponge Phone," he read.

"That's right. It's the *Sponge* Phone, not the *Pat* Phone. Kindly stand aside while I answer the call of justice." Man Sponge swept past Boy Patrick and picked up the phone.

"That's not fair," Boy Patrick grumbled, but Man Sponge didn't hear him. He was too busy answering the call of justice.

"Copy that, sir! We'll be there right away!" said Man Sponge, hanging up. "To the *Invisible Floatmobile*, Boy Patrick! Someone's in danger!"

The two action heroes raced outside and hopped into a rickety, old boat.

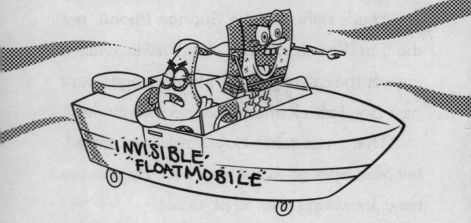

"Put the pedal to the metal, Boy Patrick! We've no time to lose!" cried Man Sponge from the passenger seat.

"But I drove *last* time," Boy Patrick complained.

"Right, you did, my crime-fighting companion. But I am Man Sponge and I must be free to keep an eye out for evil at all times."

"Somebody's getting a little too big for his superpants," Boy Patrick muttered.

A short while later, the *Invisible Floatmobile* screeched to a halt on a busy street in downtown Bikini Bottom.

"Look, over there! That citizen is in desperate need of a rescue!" Man Sponge exclaimed. He pointed to a young lady whose arms were piled high with packages.

"There's a puddle of mud in front of her and she's going to walk right through it!" Boy Patrick gasped. "We've got to help her!"

"I'll handle this, Boy Patrick!" said Man Sponge confidently. He scurried over to the puddle, flopped down on top of it, and soaked up the mud just as the young lady was about to step in it.

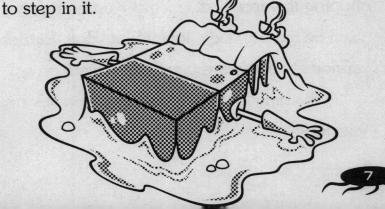

"My hero!" she cried and covered Man Sponge with kisses. "How will I ever repay you?"

"No payment necessary, ma'am. It's my duty to help citizens in need," Man Sponge told her, smiling.

"It's my duty, too," Boy Patrick added, hoping to win a kiss.

The young lady looked at Boy Patrick curiously. "Who are you?" she asked.

"Oh, him?" Man Sponge said. "He's my sidekick."

"Your sidekick? *Your* sidekick?!" Boy Patrick shouted angrily. "We're supposed to be a team! I'm tired of being your flunky, Man Sponge!"

Back in the present, SpongeBob shuddered. "It was such an awful dream, Gary! And it all seemed so real!"

"Meow," Gary replied.

"I know, Gary. Boy Patrick was so angry with me. I'm glad it was just a dream." SpongeBob breathed a sigh of relief.

"Meow!" Gary exclaimed.

"Goodness! You're right, Gary. Look at the time! I'd better get ready for work."

SpongeBob quickly took a shower, brushed his teeth, and got dressed. By the time he was ready to leave, he'd forgotten all about his bad dream. Whistling happily, he opened his front door and came face-to-face with Patrick.

"Hey there, buddy," SpongeBob greeted his friend.

But Patrick wasn't happy. He glared at SpongeBob and waved the picket sign he was holding. SpongeBob stared at the sign and gasped. It read: MAN SPONGE IS DRIED UP!

LATE FOR WORK

SpongeBob couldn't believe his eyes. He looked from Patrick to the sign, and back to Patrick again. "Gee, Pat, is that any way to treat your best friend?"

"I told you, SpongeBob. I'm tired of being your flunky!"

"My flunky? Now wait just a—" SpongeBob stopped. "Uh-oh, last night wasn't a dream, was it? It was real."

"Of course it was real!" Patrick bellowed.

"Listen, Pat—"

"No, you listen, SpongeBob. You think

that just because I'm your sidekick you can kick me around. Well I've had it! I'm tired of you taking all the glory!"

"Don't be silly, Pat. I don't take all the glory."

"Oh yeah? What about that time with the catfish?" Patrick's frown deepened as he thought back to that fateful day. . . .

Man Sponge and Boy Patrick were out patrolling the streets of Bikini Bottom when they heard a desperate cry for help.

"Help! Please, somebody help me!" a young woman cried tearfully. "It's my pet catfish. He's stuck in a patch of coral!"

Man Sponge and Boy Patrick rushed to the woman's side.

"Not to worry. I'll help you," Man Sponge told her.

Boy Patrick looked at the catfish and noticed that it was scared. "Here, kitty. Here, kitty, kitty," he whispered, hoping to coax it free.

"Nice try, Boy Patrick, but that'll never work. A situation like this calls for a much more sophisticated approach," Man Sponge explained. He stared at the trapped catfish and scratched his chin in thought. "Aha! I've got it! Watch and learn."

Man Sponge knelt down next to the coral patch and whispered, "Here, kitty. Here, kitty, kitty."

Sure enough, the catfish swished its fins and worked its way free.

"You did it! You saved my catfish! Oh, thank you, Man Sponge!" said the young woman. "That was amazing!"

"It was pretty amazing, wasn't it? I don't know where I get these ideas. It's like they just come to me," Man Sponge replied. "Well, I've got to go, miss. Duty calls."

"Those were good times," SpongeBob said when Patrick was done remembering.

"Yeah, except for the part where you stole my idea and took all the glory!" Patrick snapped.

"Look, Pat, can we talk about this later?" SpongeBob asked. "I'm late for work."

"No, SpongeBob, I'm tired of being ignored. I won't wait!" Patrick said firmly.

"Well, neither will my customers! They depend on me for Krabby Patties!" SpongeBob argued.

"Then I guess you don't have a choice," Patrick grumbled.

The two friends stared angrily at each other. Exasperated, SpongeBob began walking toward the Krusty Krab. Patrick followed, waving his sign and chanting, "Down with Man Sponge!"

SECOND BANANA

When SpongeBob and Patrick walked up to the Krusty Krab, there was a long line of customers winding all the way down the block. *I wonder what's going on*, SpongeBob thought. He rushed inside with Patrick close on his heels.

At the front of the line were two very familiar heroes—Mermaidman and Barnacleboy! They were staring at the menu board in confusion.

"Let's see, I want a . . . no . . . I'll have a . . . no . . . hmmm . . ." Mermaidman mumbled uncertainly.

"Sir, will you please order already? You're holding up the line," Squidward said, annoyed. SpongeBob leaped at the chance to help his favorite heroes. He sidled up to Mermaidman and whispered, "Psst, Mermaidman, get a Krabby Patty!"

"I've made my decision!" Mermaidman announced.

The line of customers cheered. They'd been waiting forever for him to order.

"One Krabby Patty for me and one Pipsqueak Patty for the boy, please," said Mermaidman triumphantly.

"Now wait just a minute!" Barnacleboy stamped his foot in frustration. "I don't want a Pipsqueak Patty. I want an adult-size Krabby Patty."

"The Krabby Patty is too big for you," Mermaidman told him. "You'll never finish it all."

"The boy's eyes are bigger than his stomach," chuckled Mr. Krabs. The crowd of customers laughed, which only made Barnacleboy angrier.

"And that's another thing! I'm not a boy. I'm so old I've got hairs growing out of the wrinkles on my liver spots!" Barnacleboy snapped. But it didn't matter what he said.

Squidward ducked into the kitchen and came out holding the world's tiniest patty. "One Pipsqueak Patty and your bib and high chair," he said mockingly.

Barnacleboy shook his fist in anger. "I'm sixty-eight years old and . . .

I WANT A KRABBY PATTY!"

"Your Pipsqueak is getting cold," Mermaidman said gently. He picked up the tiny patty and held it out to his friend. "Shall I feed you?"

"Feed this, old man!" Barnacleboy shouted. He knocked the Pipsqueak Patty out of Mermaidman's hand.

"Ooooooo," the crowd gasped.

"I'm tired of playing second banana to you!" Barnacleboy yelled.

"But the two of you are a team! There's no such thing as second banana!" SpongeBob said. "Mermaidman and Barnacleboy work together to rid the world of evil! Remember the time Man Ray and the Dirty Bubble invented a dastardly Freeze Ray and threatened to put all of Bikini Bottom on ice?"

Barnacleboy folded his arms across his chest and sulked.

"Well, I do," SpongeBob said. "I remember it like it was yesterday . . ."

And with that SpongeBob told the crowd all about the amazing duo that once was Mermaidman and Barnacleboy. . . .

Mermaidman and Barnacleboy were in hot pursuit of Man Ray and the Dirty Bubble.

"Stop, in the name of justice!" Mermaidman called after the villains.

"Justice? I don't see anyone here by that name," Man Ray snickered.

"Actually, Justice is my middle name," said Barnacleboy.

"Does that mean we have to stop?" the Dirty Bubble whispered to Man Ray.

"Keep moving," Man Ray said. "A few more steps and we'll have them within position of our Freeze Ray!"

"We've got you now, fiends!" cried Mermaidman.

"Surrender or we'll— Do you hear that Barnacleboy?"

"Hear what? This is no time to hesitate. Man Ray and the Dirty Bubble are about to escape!" said Barnacleboy.

Just then, an ice-cream truck rolled past playing a catchy little tune.

"Ice cream? I love ice cream!" Mermaidman exclaimed. He broke off from chasing the villains and ran after the ice-cream truck.

"So, you like ice cream, do you?" Man Ray snarled. "One blast from our Freeze Ray and all of Bikini Bottom will be on ice!"

The Dirty Bubble turned to Man Ray and whispered, "What are we going to do once the whole town is frozen?"

"Not sure yet, but we're villains, we'll figure it out," Man Ray replied. He switched on the Freeze Ray and turned it toward Mermaidman and the ice-cream truck.

"What are you waiting for?" asked the Dirty Bubble. "Fire away!"

"I can't," said Man Ray. "It has to heat up."

"It's a Freeze Ray and it has to heat up? Oh, for Neptune's sake!" The Dirty Bubble looked ready to burst.

"Do you have prune with bran sprinkles? It's my favorite. Keeps me regular," Mermaidman told the ice-cream truck driver.

"Put down that cone, Mermaidman! There's evil at work!" Barnacleboy shouted.

"*EVIL?*" Mermaidman bellowed. "I hate evil!"

"You sure do," said Barnacleboy. "Now, why don't you use that utility belt of yours and help us capture these criminals!"

"That's right, Barnacleboy!" Mermaidman punched a button on his utility belt and blasted Man Ray and the Dirty Bubble with his Small

Ray. The two villains shrank rapidly until they were no bigger than the tiniest plankton. Barnacleboy scooped them up in his hand and dropped them into his pocket.

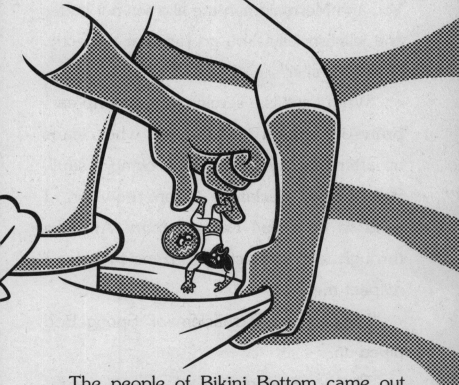

The people of Bikini Bottom came out of their houses and cheered, "Hooray for Mermaidman! Hooray for Barnacleboy!"

"Hooray!" SpongeBob said, getting caught up in his own memory. Back in the present he turned to Barnacleboy. "You never would have nabbed those villains without each other. You and Mermaidman are like sea-nut butter and jellyfish jelly! You go together perfectly. Don't you see?"

"What I see is a senile old man who eats prune ice cream and the sap who cleans up after him. Well, I'm done being a sap!" Barnacleboy declared. "From now on, I want to be called Barnacle*man*! And I'm through with protecting citizens that don't respect me!"

"*I* respect you, Barnacleman!" SpongeBob piped up.

"That's Barnacle*boy*! I mean, *man*. Ooooh, forget you people! I say, if you're not going to give me any respect as a hero, then maybe you'll give me respect as a villain!

A villain who is . . .

EVIL!"

Barnacleman roared.

"Evil?" SpongeBob gasped.

"Evil?" Mr. Krabs and Patrick cried in unison.

"EVIL?" Mermaidman bellowed.

"That's right! I'm crossing over to the dark side," Barnacleman announced. He pointed to the opposite side of the room. It was pitch black.

"What? Why should I waste money lighting the whole store?" Mr. Krabs asked sheepishly.

Suddenly, a sleek boatmobile cruised out of the darkness. The door slid open to reveal two of Bikini Bottom's most notorious criminals.

THE DARK SIDE

Man Ray poked his head out of the window, an evil grin forming on his face. "Did someone say *evil*?"

"I did!" Barnacleman answered. "As in, sign me up!"

"Holy oil spill! It's Mermaidman and Barnacleboy's archenemies, Man Ray and the Dirty Bubble!" SpongeBob exclaimed.

"Not so fast," said Man Ray. "The last time I checked, we were enemies."

"Archenemies," SpongeBob corrected him.

"Quite right, archenemies," Man Ray

agreed. "So why should we let you join us?"

"Well, he doesn't eat much," Squidward said dryly, "just a Pipsqueak Patty every now and then."

"I've had just about enough of your lip, mister!" Barnacleman growled at Squidward.

"Oooo, he's feisty. I say we take him," said the Dirty Bubble.

"You may be right, my filthy friend," Man Ray replied. "He might be a welcome addition to our plan for world domination, since the last plan didn't go so well."

Man Ray remembered the last time their efforts to rule the world failed. . . .

At long last Man Ray and the Dirty Bubble had Mermaidman and Barnacleboy in their clutches! The two heroic do-gooders were tied back-to-back. Above them loomed a mysterious contraption built of bowling pins, vacuum cleaner hoses, old shoes, rusty pipes, and various other odds and ends, casting a menacing shadow over the superduo.

"World domination here we come!" said Man Ray.

"I can't wait!" the Dirty Bubble replied. "I'm absolutely exhausted! Who knew mayhem could be so tiring! As soon as we rule the world I'm going on vacation."

"I hear the Indian Ocean is lovely this time of year," Man Ray suggested.

"Really? I was thinking the Bay of Biscay—"

"Sorry to interrupt," Mermaidman cut in, "but you're forgetting the one thing standing between you and your vacation."

"The rainy season? Oh, you're right. Last year the Atomic Flounder and I went to the Caribbean in the middle of July and almost got washed away! Never again!" the Dirty Bubble exclaimed.

"Not the rainy season! *Us!*" Mermaidman cried. "You'll have to go through us!"

"Yeah!" Barnacleboy seconded. He glanced up at the bizarre device that hung over them. "So your wicked plan is to . . . junk us into submission?"

"Junk? This isn't junk! What you see above you is a masterpiece!" Man Ray declared. "A brilliant display of criminal genius!"

"That's right!" said the Dirty Bubble. "Uh, how does it work again?" he asked Man Ray.

"Simple. I turn this crank here, which draws back the boot, which kicks the pipe, which rattles the cage, which knocks the pin that loosens the net, which drops from the hook, and falls on the clam that chews through the rope . . ."

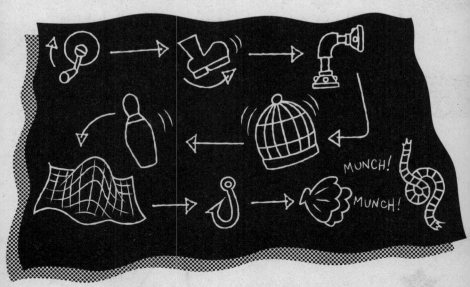

As Man Ray's explanation went on and on, Mermaidman and Barnacleboy tried to think of a way out. In an effort to free himself from the ropes around his arms, Barnacleboy accidentally elbowed Mermaidman in the side, which caused him to shout out in pain. This, then, reminded him that a shout was all it would take to free them both. "Sea creatures! UNITE!" he cried out.

The ocean rippled all around them. Man Ray was almost finished explaining his machine when a mass of fish, dolphins, clams, and seahorses swam toward them. The sea creatures nibbled through Mermaidman and Barnacleboy's ropes, freeing them.

"Thank you, friends!" said Mermaidman. "Now, how'd you like a closer look at a masterpiece?" Following his command, the sea creatures turned to Man Ray's machine. They bumped and butted it with their bodies until it was nothing more than a pile of rubble.

"Noooooooo!" Man Ray shouted.

"Foiled again!" cried the Dirty Bubble in defeat.

Returning from his reverie, Man Ray concluded: "And we would have won if you could've controlled your limbs, Barnacleman!"

"All the more reason to have him on our side," the Dirty Bubble reminded his partner.

"Agreed. Welcome to Team E.V.I.L., Barnacleman," said Man Ray.

Barnacleman hopped into the villains' boat and sneered at Mermaidman. "Nighty night, you old goat!" He slammed the door and the boat sped off.

"Nighty night," Mermaidman replied. "Will you tuck me in?" he asked SpongeBob. Unfortunately, SpongeBob was too stunned to reply. The world's most famous crime-fighting team had just split up! It was too awful for words!

Then, things went from bad to worse.

"I'm joining the dark side, too," Patrick

announced. "Take that, Man Sponge!" He walked across the room and stood on the dark side of the restaurant.

Five seconds later . . .

"Um, it's dark over here," Patrick whined. "Anybody got a light?"

Squidward sighed in exasperation. "The villains left already, Patrick! It's too late to join them."

"Oh, right. I knew that." Patrick looked sheepish. He came back to the lit side of the restaurant and stood next to Mr. Krabs.

Moments later a voice rang out. "We interrupt your bleak and meaningless lives for this special news break!"

E.V.I.L.

SpongeBob, Patrick, Sandy, Squidward, and Mr. Krabs all looked up at the TV hanging over the front counter for a special news bulletin.

The news announcer continued, "Man Ray, the Dirty Bubble, and now playing for the dark side, Barnacleboy—"

"Barnacle*man*!" shouted Barnacleman from the TV screen.

"—have been committing a series of crimes throughout Bikini Bottom," the news

announcer explained.

SpongeBob watched the news footage in horror. Man Ray, the Dirty Bubble, and Barnacleman were wreaking havoc all over town. SpongeBob covered his eyes! He couldn't bear to look! But seconds later his curiosity got the best of him. He peeked through his fingers only to see the three criminals pull the worst prank of all. They ran up to a house, rang the doorbell, and then ran away!

"I'll get you crazy kids!" shouted the old man who answered the door.

The villains snickered as they ran off to cause more trouble.

Back at the news desk, the announcer continued. "These three criminals have named their new alliance Every Villain Is Lemons . . . otherwise known as E.V.I.L.! What can we do?

When will this crime wave end? How will we defeat the evil? Why am I asking you all these questions? Mermaidman, where are you?"

Mermaidman had dozed off. Mr. Krabs swatted him with a claw, jolting him awake. "I'm right here!" said Mermaidman. "Don't worry, good citizens! Nothing will stop me from defeating evil . . . nothing!"

Mermaidman ran out of the Krusty Krab hot on the trail of evil. Suddenly, he heard a familiar sound. An ice-cream truck rolled into view.

"Ice cream! I love ice cream!" he said, forgetting all about evil. "A double scoop of prune with bran sprinkles!"

A mysterious gloved hand snaked out from the window and handed Mermaidman his ice-cream cone.

Mermaidman took one lick and the cone exploded. "Goes right through me every time," he said, stunned.

Just then, he heard an evil laugh.

Barnacleman leaned out of the ice-cream truck with Man Ray and the Dirty Bubble at his side. "You might as well give it up, old man. There are three of us and only one of you. You don't stand a chance!" Barnacleman gloated. He took the wheel of the ice-cream truck and drove off, tires squealing.

"Mermaidman, are you all right?" SpongeBob asked as he came running up.

Patrick, Sandy, and Squidward were right behind him. "Oh, how are you going to beat all three of those guys by yourself?"

Mermaidman's shoulders slumped. "You're right. I give up." He flopped down on the ground.

"You can't give up! What if we help you?" SpongeBob suggested.

"That's a terrible idea," Mermaidman said grumpily. "Wait, I've got it!" He snapped his fingers. "What if you help me?"

"Okay," SpongeBob agreed.

"So, who wants to save the world?" Mermaidman asked.

"I do!" SpongeBob answered eagerly.

"I do!" said Sandy.

"I do!" Patrick cried.

"I don't," Squidward grumbled.

"Oh, yes you do!" said Mr. Krabs as he scuttled up to them. "No world means no money." He told Squidward. "Now go save the world or you're fired."

"That's settled then," said Mermaidman brightly. "To the Mermalair!"

THE I.J.L.S.A.

"Wow, the Mermalair!" SpongeBob marveled, as he, Patrick, Sandy, and Squidward followed Mermaidman into the headquarters of Bikini Bottom's most famous action heroes. It was full of crime-fighting gadgets, inventions, and devices—not to mention the smell of justice wafting through its halls.

They walked past a row of costumes, each one enclosed in its own glass case.

"These costumes belong to the original International Justice League of Super Acquaintances," explained Mermaidman.

49

"Wow! The I.J.L.S.A. were the most heroic heroes ever! And you had the best lunchbox, too," SpongeBob said to Mermaidman.

"The I.J.L.S.A. did more than just look good on a lunchbox. We were an unstoppable team of crime-fighting equals!"

"Equals?" Patrick perked up. "You mean, like nobody was a flunky?"

"That's right, Peter," Mermaidman replied.

And you all took turns driving the boatmobile?" asked Patrick. He cut SpongeBob a knowing look.

"Right again, Pedro! We were a team," said Mermaidman. "Why, I remember this one time . . ."

Mermaidman thought back to the famous bank heist that the I.J.L.S.A. had thwarted. . . .

Mermaidman and his fellow Super Acquaintances—the Quickster, Captain Magma, the Elastic Waistband, and Miss Appear—were all gathered at the Mermalair when the phone rang.

"I'll get it," said Mermaidman, picking up the receiver. "Hello? Oh, hey there, chief. What's that you say? A robbery? Not to worry! We'll be right there!" Mermaidman hung up. "Super Acquaintances, to the *Invisible Boatmobile!*"

The superfriends ran through the Mermalair to the secret cavern where they kept their boat. Mermaidman was the first to arrive. He unlocked the *Invisible Boatmobile* and held open the door for his crime-fighting companions. "After you," he said.

"No, after you," said the Quickster.

"No, after you," Mermaidman replied.

"Really, I insist," the Quickster said.

"Don't be silly, we're all equals here," Mermaidman pointed out.

"Then ladies first," the Quickster said to Miss Appear.

"Oh no, I couldn't," Miss Appear replied. "After you, Captain Magma."

"I think the Waistband should go first," Captain Magma said.

"No, after you," said the Elastic Waistband.

Five minutes later, the Super Acquaintances

had finally piled into the *Invisible Boatmobile*. They took off, headed for Bikini Bottom National Bank.

When they got to the scene, they saw two criminals running out of the bank with bags of money.

"I'll stop them!" cried Mermaidman. "Unless you want to, Waistband."

"No, no," said the Elastic Waistband. "You go right ahead."

"Are you sure?" asked Mermaidman.

"I'm positive. Unless it's Magma's turn."

"I just thwarted a crime yesterday," Captain Magma replied. "Really, it's up to the Quickster to keep our streets safe."

"I wouldn't feel right," said the Quickster. "Not when Miss Appear is just as worthy as I am."

"Oh, stop your sweet talk, Quickster." Miss Appear chuckled.

"Well, someone needs to stop them!" cried an innocent bystander.

"You're right!" said Mermaidman. "Super Acquaintances, unite!"

The Quickster used his superspeed to run circles around the thieves. He ran so fast that he made them dizzy.

Next, Miss Appear turned herself invisible. She sneaked up to the dizzy bandits and slipped the money bags out of their hands. They never even saw her coming!

"What's going on?" asked the first villain, scared.

"I don't know," his partner in crime answered. "Forget the money! Let's get out of here, man."

The criminals made a break for it, but Mermaidman pelted them with water balls. Then, the Elastic Waistband used his amazing powers of elasticity to stretch himself into a long, thin rope. He wrapped himself around the criminals and kept them tied up until the police arrived.

Once again, the Super Acquaintances had saved the day!

"That's incredible!" said SpongeBob when Mermaidman had finished his story.

"It sure is," Mermaidman agreed. "And now I'm giving you the chance to join me and form a new league of Super Acquaintances!" He touched a button and lowered the glass cases surrounding the costumes. "Now, who's with me?"

KRACK-A-TOWA!

SpongeBob shot Patrick a nervous glance. "Just a second, Mermaidman," he said, pulling Patrick aside.

"What are we going to do?" SpongeBob whispered urgently to Patrick. "This is our chance to be part of a legendary team of crime-fighters!"

"Yeah, a real team of equals!" Patrick said dreamily.

"But what about Man Sponge and Boy Patrick?"

"What about them?" Patrick asked.

"If we put on these costumes we'll have to give them up. We can't be both!"

Patrick frowned. "I hadn't thought about that."

"It's true, Patrick! What are we going to do? I can't just stop being Man Sponge. Remember the day we first became super crime-fighters?"

"Like it was yesterday," Patrick replied. "It all started when you were bit by the rabid clam."

"Huh?" SpongeBob said.

"You know, that rabid clam. We thought something

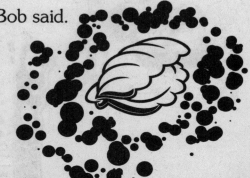

was wrong with it 'cause it was glowing in the dark. Then it just hopped up and snapped you right on the nose."

"Patrick, that's not how it—"

"Then the next day you started to feel funny, and that's when you discovered your special powers, like the power to see real good and the power to make Krabby Patties—"

"Patrick—"

"'From this day forth, I shall call myself Man Sponge,' you said. 'Huzzah!'"

SpongeBob thought about interrupting again, but decided against it. Patrick was on a roll.

"Then there was the birth of Boy Patrick, who came to earth in a meteor shower as a tiny baby," Patrick said. "He was raised in

a small farm town outside of Bikini Bottom and draws his powers from the Dutchman's golden spatula!"

"WHOSOEVER HOLDS THIS SPATULA, IF HE BE WORTHY, SHALL POSSESS THE POWER OF... THE DUTCHMAN"

"Patrick!" SpongeBob couldn't contain himself any longer. "That's not what happened!"

"It's not?"

"No, I think you're confusing us with other heroes."

"I am?"

"Yes."

"Then what really happened?" asked Patrick.

"Well, we were going to go jellyfishing but we found holes in our nets, remember? So we decided to do arts and crafts at my house," SpongeBob explained.

"And that's when the rabid clam bit you!" Patrick gasped.

"No, Pat. There was no rabid clam. We made masks out of construction paper and spent the afternoon picking out super names."

"That's it?" Patrick asked.

SpongeBob nodded, tears welling at the corners of his eyes as he thought about that special day.

"If you two are done strolling down memory lane, I'd like to get this show on the road," Mermaidman said. "It's almost time for my nap."

"What do we have to do?" SpongeBob looked anxious.

"Just put on these costumes and the fantastic powers of the International Justice League of Super Acquaintances will become yours!" Mermaidman explained.

"Wow! I didn't think superpowers worked that way," Sandy said.

"Sure. The power is all in the costume," Mermaidman told them. "Why else would we run around in colored undies?"

"Wait a minute," said SpongeBob. "You

mean these costumes come with *real* superpowers?"

"That's right, Bucky," Mermaidman replied.

SpongeBob and Patrick exchanged a glance. They could still be Man Sponge and Boy Patrick when they switched costumes. "Count us in!" they said together.

"Excellent!" cried Mermaidman. "Let's get everyone into their outfits."

A short while later, the new I.J.L.S.A. emerged wearing their costumes. SpongeBob was absolutely thrilled. He imagined the news reporting on this momentous event. . . .

"Breaking news!" said the imaginary announcer. "We go live to the Mermalair where a new International Justice League of Super Acquaintances has just been formed. Here they are now!"

SpongeBob waved to the imaginary camera in his shiny Quickster uniform.

"The Quickster! With the uncanny ability to run really quick!" said the newscaster.

"Want to see me run to that mountain and back?" SpongeBob asked. He moved so quickly it looked like he was standing still.

"Captain Magma! Get him angry and he's bound to erupt!" announced the newscaster.

"KRACK-A-TOWA!"

Squidward shouted, shooting flames from Magma's fiery helmet.

"The Elastic Waistband," the newscaster cried, "able to stretch his body into fantastic shapes and forms!"

"I can finally touch my toes!" Patrick exclaimed, using the waistband's powers to twist himself into a pretzel.

"And Miss Appear! Now you see her, now you don't," the newscaster said. Sandy stepped forward in Miss Appear's costume and suddenly faded from view. "Does this outfit make me look fat?" she asked.

"The International Justice League of Super Acquaintances, a subsidiary of Viacom," the announcer concluded.

When SpongeBob came back to reality, Mermaidman had fallen asleep. SpongeBob shook him gently.

Mermaidman's eyes sprang open. "Gather around, Super Acquaintances," he said. "We've got work to do."

MAKE-OUT REEF

Later at the Mermalair, the I.J.L.S.A. was in the middle of some very important business.

"So it's agreed," Mermaidman said, "we'll get one cheese pizza, one with pepperoni and mushrooms, and one with olives."

Suddenly, the video screen on the wall lit up.

"Super Acquaintances, we need your help!" someone cried.

"Holy halibut! It's the chief!" the Quickster said.

"Thank you for the introduction, Quickster,

but we all know who I am. More to the point, we've got news on the whereabouts of E.V.I.L.," the chief explained.

"The whoseabouts of what?" asked the Elastic Waistband.

"You just tell us where they are, chief, and we'll hogtie 'em faster than you can say 'salsa verde,'" Miss Appear promised.

"Our sources last saw E.V.I.L. harassing some teenagers up at Make-Out Reef! You know, Make-Out Reef. Woo-hoo! Mwah! Mwah!" said the chief, making kissing noises.

"Floppin' flounder, Mermaidman! Make-Out Reef!" The Quickster gasped.

"Those fiends!" cried Mermaidman.

"Ah, Make-Out Reef! Good times, good times." Captain Magma chuckled softly to himself.

"To Make-Out Reef! AWAY!" called Mermaidman.

"Does this mean we're not getting pizza?" the Elastic Waistband asked sadly.

Meanwhile, at Make-Out Reef, the super villains known as E.V.I.L. were doing their best to pester teenagers.

Man Ray, the Dirty Bubble, and
Barnacleman taunted a pair of teenagers
parked in a boat. "John and Nancy sittin' in a
tree, K-I-S-S-I-N-G!" they chanted, shining a
flashlight on them.

"Leave us alone!" the young couple cried.
The villains laughed mischievously.

"Shine the flashlight in that car over there,
Man Ray!" the Dirty Bubble urged his partner
in crime.

"With pleasure," Man Ray replied. He shined the flashlight on another parked car. The light revealed a lonely boy inside kissing a pillow.

"Hey, man, that's not cool," the boy complained.

The three criminals snickered. They hadn't had this much fun in ages!

Just then, Mermaidman arrived to put an end to their laughter. "Leave those young kids alone!" he cried.

"Well, if it isn't Milkmaidman. You saved us the trouble of tracking you down," Man Ray hissed.

"You fiends can't win. You're out-numbered!" Mermaidman shouted.

"You senile bag of fish paste! There are three of us and only one of you," Man Ray growled.

"Make that two!" called the Quickster as he raced to Mermaidman's side.

"Three!" Captain Magma rocketed onto the scene.

"Four!" The Elastic Waistband stretched to join his friends.

"Five!" cried Miss Appear, suddenly visible.

"And me makes ten," Mermaidman said, counting on his fingers. "I think."

"Uh-oh, I don't feel so good about this," the Dirty Bubble said nervously. In fact, all three supervillains looked worried.

"Well, there goes our big toy deal!" Barnacleman sighed.

"Super Acquaintances, attack!" Mermaidman shouted.

"No! Please! Mercy!" cried Barnacleman. He and the alliance of E.V.I.L. were quaking in their boots.

"Krack-a-towa!" Captain Magma shouted. A burst of flaming lava shot out from the top of his fiery helmet. Unfortunately, instead of landing on the criminals, it plopped down on top of the Quickster's head.

"AHHHHH! AHHHH! GET IT OFF! GET IT OFF! GET IT OFF!"

the Quickster screamed. Panicked, he ran in a circle trying to shake off the burning lava.

"I'll save you, Quickster!" said the Elastic Waistband. He took off after his friend. What happened next wasn't pretty. The Quickster was moving really fast—so fast that the Elastic Waistband's rubbery arms and legs got tangled up in his wake.

"I'll cool you off, Quickster, with one of my water balls!" Mermaidman said. By this time the Quickster was running so fast he was a blur. Mermaidman squinted trying to see him. He launched a water ball, but it accidentally landed on Captain Magma instead.

"Noooo!" Captain Magma cried, as the water ball doused his flames and reduced him to ashes.

"Well, I guess it's up to me," said Miss Appear. She became invisible and began creeping toward the criminals. "I'll just sneak over, unseen, and catch them by surprise," she whispered. Unfortunately for Miss Appear, the criminals weren't the only ones who couldn't see her. Suddenly, she was hit by a passing boat and knocked off a cliff! The driver had no idea she was there!

"Get it off! Get it off!" The Quickster was still aflame and running in circles. At last the lava burned out, but there was nothing left of the Quickster except two smoking shoes.

Mermaidman took one look at the sad state of the Super Acquaintances and fell over.

Man Ray, the Dirty Bubble, and Barnacleman stared at one another in shock. They had gone from being outnumbered to defeating a legendary crime-fighting team without lifting a finger.

"We did it! We won! The day belongs to E.V.I.L.!" Barnacleman said triumphantly.

UH, WORLD DOMINATION?

Barnacleman gloated. "Heh, heh, heh! You've lost, Mermaidman. And the hero-villain rules say you have to give in to my demands."

Mermaidman knelt down in front of Barnacleman. "Okay, what do you want?"

"World domination! Tell him we want world domination!" Man Ray said eagerly.

"And make him eat dirt!" the Dirty Bubble added.

"Number one: I want to be treated like an equal, not a sidekick," Barnacleman began. "Number two: I want to be called Barnacleman. And number three . . ."

"Come on, world domination!" Man Ray chimed in, fingers crossed.

"I want an adult-size Krabby Patty," Barnacleman finished.

The Dirty Bubble turned to Man Ray. "Did you hear him say anything about eating dirt?" he asked.

Mermaidman nodded, accepting the demands.

Barnacleman smiled. "Need a hand, Super Pal?" He reached out to Mermaidman and helped him get to his feet.

"Good to have you back on the side of justice, Kyle," said Mermaidman. "Let's go get you that Krabby Patty."

"Was that it?" asked Man Ray, thoroughly disappointed.

"No." Man Ray heard an unexpected voice. In his torn Elastic Waistband costume, Patrick gathered up his rubbery limbs and dragged them over to SpongeBob. "I've got some demands too."

"Oh, goody!" said the Dirty Bubble.

"Is it even worth me saying world domination again?" Man Ray asked dryly.

SpongeBob shook off the ashes of his Quickster outfit. "What do you want, Pat?"

"Well, number one: I don't want to always drive the *Invisible Floatmobile*," Patrick said.

"Okay, we'll take turns," SpongeBob agreed.

"Number two: I want to answer the phone when justice calls."

"But it's the Sponge Phone!"

Patrick raised an angry eyebrow.

"Fine," SpongeBob said. "I guess we can call it the Sponge–Pat Phone."

Patrick nodded. "And number three: Now that I've seen what it's like to be on a team of equals, no more second banana."

"Pat, you were never second banana.

I'm sorry if the whole superduo thing kinda went to my head. But I know I couldn't do it without you. We're a team! We go together like . . ."

"Sea-nut butter and jellyfish jelly?" Barnacleman suggested.

"Just like sea-nut butter and jellyfish jelly!" SpongeBob said. "Friends?" He reached out a hand to Patrick.

"Friends," Patrick agreed. He shook SpongeBob's hand and pulled him into a bear hug.

"Oh, for Neptune's sake!" cried Man Ray. "Will no one demand world domination?"

OH, PIPSQUEAK!

Later at the Krusty Krab, Mermaidman and Barnacleman were once again standing at the front of the line. This time, though, they knew exactly what to order.

"That'll be two Krabby Patties, please," said Mermaidman. "One for me and one for my . . . equal."

SpongeBob and Patrick watched as the two legendary crime-fighters carried their Krabby Patties to a table and sat down to eat lunch together.

"It does me good to see those two back

together again," said SpongeBob.

"Me too," Patrick replied.

"But there is one thing I'm kinda sad about."

"What's that?"

SpongeBob leaned forward and whispered, "I really miss being the Quickster."

"I know!" Patrick agreed.

"When I was the Waistband, I got to be all rubbery."

"I mean, Man Sponge is the greatest, but he's not as fast as the Quickster. No one is," SpongeBob said with a glint in his eye. "Those superpowers were *real*."

Patrick nodded. "Who knew they came with the costume? I always thought you had to get bitten by a rabid clam."

"Well, I guess we just have to settle for what we have," SpongeBob said sadly.

"Maybe not," Patrick replied. "Maybe we can make up our own superpowers."

"Patrick! That's a brilliant idea!"

"Ooooo, I know what mine is," Patrick said. "I have the power to sleep with my eyes open!"

"And I, Man Sponge, am the world's best trash picker-upper!" SpongeBob announced.

"I think it's time for us to test out our new superpowers. To the Sponge Lair, AWAY!"

SpongeBob and Patrick dashed across the restaurant. On their way out they heard their favorite heroes deep in conversation.

"How's that adult-size Krabby Patty treating you, Barnacleman?" Mermaidman asked.

"Actually, it's pretty big. I'm not sure I can finish the whole thing," Barnacleman replied.

Mermaidman stared at his friend for a moment and then burst out laughing. Barnacleman laughed, too. It wasn't long before the whole restaurant was laughing with them, remembering the Pipsqueak Patty that started it all.

THE END

OH, TARTAR SAUCE!

SpongeBob struck a manly pose. "Come, Boy Patrick! While our heroes are away, we will keep evil at bay!"

He jumped deeper into the cave, flipping and making karate sounds.

Patrick followed, kicking the air with his pink legs.

But as he turned a corner in the cave, Patrick spotted something that made him freeze in his tracks. Trembling, he tried to tell SpongeBob what he saw. "M-m-m-m-m . . ."

SpongeBob heard Patrick and came back to where he stood, shaking with fear. "What is it, trusted sidekick?" he asked.

Patrick still couldn't get out the words. "M-m-m-m . . ."

SpongeBob peered into a cavernous chamber and saw what had frightened Patrick. Shuddering, he couldn't get out the words either. "M-m-m-m . . ."

They clung to each other, terrified. Finally they managed to force out the words they'd been trying to say to each other.

"MAN RAY!!!"

The evil supervillain stood in a dark room, stretching his gloved hands toward SpongeBob and Patrick.

"AAAHH!!"

they screamed, dashing away.

SpongeBob realized Man Ray wasn't chasing them. He tiptoed back to meet Patrick. "How come he's not chasing us, Man Sponge?" Patrick asked.

Man Sponge decided he needed to investigate further. He took a deep breath to calm himself and crept toward Man Ray. The villain stood absolutely still, not making a sound.

"Looks like he's frozen or something, Boy Patrick."

Patrick shivered, muttering, "Fro-fro-fro-fro-fro-fro . . ."

Man Sponge fearlessly approached Man Ray, until he could see that the villain was inside a column of cold, white goo. Knocking on the column, he said, "It appears to be some sort of prison chamber . . ."—he licked the goo—"made out of frozen tartar sauce!"

SpongeBob stood back admiring the tartar-sauce trap. "This is incredible! Next to the Dirty Bubble, the evil Man Ray is the all-time greatest arch-nemesis of Mermaidman and Barnacleboy. I have so many questions to ask him!"

At that very moment, the tartar sauce holding Man Ray started to melt. Laughing goofily, Patrick stood by a control switch he had flipped from FREEZE to UNFREEZE.

SpongeBob ran over to Patrick. "Pat, what are you doing? We're not supposed to touch anything!"

Patrick looked puzzled. "But you said you had a question."

"We could get in trouble!" SpongeBob cried.

"That's not a question," answered Patrick.

While they argued, the tartar sauce melted down past Man Ray's head. His eyes glowed a menacing red.

"They said not to touch anything and that includes unfreezing a supervillain," SpongeBob insisted.

Then, from above their heads, came a low, evil voice. "I'm FREE!" it gloated, laughing a horrible laugh!